# It's Thanksgiving!

*Dear Parent:*
*Your child's love of reading starts here!*

Every child learns to read in a different way and at his or her own speed. Some go back and forth between reading levels and read favorite books again and again. Others read through each level in order. You can help your young reader improve and become more confident by encouraging his or her own interests and abilities. From books your child reads with you to the first books he or she reads alone, there are I Can Read Books for every stage of reading:

**SHARED READING**
Basic language, word repetition, and whimsical illustrations, ideal for sharing with your emergent reader

**BEGINNING READING**
Short sentences, familiar words, and simple concepts for children eager to read on their own

**READING WITH HELP**
Engaging stories, longer sentences, and language play for developing readers

**READING ALONE**
Complex plots, challenging vocabulary, and high-interest topics for the independent reader

**ADVANCED READING**
Short paragraphs, chapters, and exciting themes for the perfect bridge to chapter books

I Can Read Books have introduced children to the joy of reading since 1957. Featuring award-winning authors and illustrators and a fabulous cast of beloved characters, I Can Read Books set the standard for beginning readers.

A lifetime of discovery begins with the magical words "I Can Read!"

*Visit www.icanread.com for information*
*on enriching your child's reading experience.*

# It's Thanksgiving!

*For my brother*
*—J.P.*

*For Abby, Jennifer, and Amanda*
*—M.H.*

ISBN-13: 978-0-545-10985-7
ISBN-10: 0-545-10985-X

Text copyright © 1982, 2007 by Jack Prelutsky.
Illustrations copyright © 1982, 2007 by Marylin Hafner. All rights reserved.
Published by Scholastic Inc., 557 Broadway, New York, NY 10012, by arrangement with HarperCollins Children's Books, a division of HarperCollins Publishers. I CAN READ BOOK® is a trademark of HarperCollins Publishers Inc. SCHOLASTIC and associated logos are trademarks and/or registered trademarks of Scholastic Inc.

12 11 10 9 8 7 6 5 4 3 2 1                    8 9 10 11 12 13/0

Printed in the U.S.A.                         23

First Scholastic printing, September 2008

# I Can Read!

# It's Thanksgiving!

by Jack Prelutsky
Children's Poet Laureate

pictures by
Marylin Hafner

SCHOLASTIC INC.
New York  Toronto  London  Auckland  Sydney
Mexico City  New Delhi  Hong Kong  Buenos Aires

# Contents

# It's Happy Thanksgiving

It's happy Thanksgiving,
Thanksgiving! Hooray!
We're going to dinner
at Grandma's today.
I love it at Grandma's,
it's cozy and snug,
I love giving Grandma
a Thanksgiving hug.

I help make the gravy,

I pour and I stir,

it smells so delicious,

I love helping her.

We laugh and we talk,

oh! she makes such a fuss

as she bustles about

cooking dinner for us.

When we sit at the table
and Daddy says grace,
there's a beautiful smile
on my grandmother's face.

Though the weather is windy
and chilly and gray,
our family is happy
this Thanksgiving day.

# The First Thanksgiving

When the Pilgrims

first gathered together to share

with their Indian friends

in the mild autumn air,

they lifted their voices

in jubilant praise

for the bread on the table,

the berries and maize,

for field and for forest,

for turkey and deer,

for the bountiful crops

they were blessed with that year.

They were thankful for these
as they feasted away,
and as they were thankful,
we're thankful today.

# The Middle of November

It's the middle of November
and the weather's crisp and cool,
Thanksgiving's getting closer
so there's lots to do at school.
Our teacher gives us projects
that we work on every day,
we make Indians and Pilgrims
out of paper, paste, and clay.

Our bright Thanksgiving murals
are displayed on all the walls,
and our cut-out paper pumpkins
gaily decorate the halls.

20

Today I drew a turkey
with a fat and funny face—
in the middle of November
school's a very busy place.

# If Turkeys Thought

If turkeys thought, they'd run away
a week before Thanksgiving Day,
but turkeys can't anticipate,
and so there's turkey on my plate.

# I Went Hungry
# on Thanksgiving

I was hungry on Thanksgiving,

but I couldn't eat a thing,

I couldn't eat a drumstick

and I couldn't eat a wing,

I couldn't have the pickles

or the gravy-covered rice,

the pumpkin pie was luscious,

but I couldn't have a slice.


I was starving for some stuffing

or a tasty yellow yam,

or a puffy little muffin

spread with homemade berry jam.

Our dinner looked delicious,

but I didn't dare to touch,

I went hungry on Thanksgiving—

my new braces hurt so much.

# The Thanksgiving Day Parade

Thanksgiving Day is here today,
the great parade is under way,
and though it's drizzling quite a bit,
I'm sure that I'll see all of it.

Great balloons are floating by,
cartoon creatures stories high,
Mickey Mouse and Mother Goose,
Snoopy and a mammoth moose.

Humpty Dumpty, Smokey Bear
hover in the autumn air,
through the windy skies they sway,
I hope that they don't blow away.

Here comes Santa, shaking hands
as he waddles by the stands.
It's so much fun, I don't complain
when now it *really* starts to rain.

The bands are marching, here they come,

pipers pipe and drummers drum,

hear the tubas and the flutes,

see the clowns in silly suits.

It's pouring now, but not on me,

I'm just as dry as I can be,

I watch and watch, but don't get wet,

I'm watching on our TV set.

# When Daddy Carves the Turkey

When Daddy carves the turkey,
it is really quite a sight,
I know he tries his hardest,
but he never does it right.

He makes a fancy show of it
before he starts to carve,
and stabs in all directions
while we're certain that we'll starve.

He seems to take forever
as we sit and shake our heads,
by the time he's finished slicing
he's reduced the bird to shreds.

He yells as loud as thunder
just before he's finally through
for when Daddy carves the turkey,
Daddy carves his finger too.

GOOD
AS
NEW!

# I Ate Too Much

I ate too much turkey,

I ate too much corn,

I ate too much pudding and pie,

I'm stuffed up with muffins

and much too much stuffin',

I'm probably going to die.

I piled up my plate

and I ate and I ate,

but I wish I had known when to stop,

for I'm so crammed with yams,

sauces, gravies, and jams

that my buttons are starting to pop.

I'm full of tomatoes

and french fried potatoes,

my stomach is swollen and sore,

but there's still some dessert,

so I guess it won't hurt

if I eat just a little bit more.

# Daddy's Football Game

Our turkey dinner's hardly gone

when Daddy says, "The game is on."

He tunes it in, takes off his shoes,

and turns to watch his heroes lose.


He seems to take it very hard

whenever they fall short a yard.

"Another incomplete," he grunts,

"more penalties, more bungled punts."

"They're missing tackles," Daddy mumbles,
"dropping passes, making fumbles. . . .
INTERCEPTION!" Daddy roars,
as once again the wrong team scores.

He sits and screams, we sit and grin,
he gets so mad when they don't win.
Thanksgiving wouldn't be the same
without my father's football game.

# The Wishbone

Wishbone, wishbone

on a dish,

pick it up

and make a wish.

If I pull

the wishbone right,

I will get

my wish tonight.

Wishbone, wishbone,

will I win?

Will I laugh

and clap and grin?

When the wishbone

snaps in two,

will my wishbone

wish come true?

Wishbone, wishbone,

now it snaps,

my sister grins

and laughs and claps.

Wishbone, wishbone,

I don't laugh,

my sister got

the bigger half.

# Gobble Gobble

When the turkey gobble gobbles,

it is plump and proud and perky.

When our family gobble gobbles,

we are gobbling down the turkey.

# Leftovers

Thanksgiving has been over
for at least a week or two,
but we're still all eating turkey,
turkey salad, turkey stew,

turkey puffs and turkey pudding,
turkey patties, turkey pies,
turkey bisque and turkey burgers,
turkey fritters, turkey fries.

For lunch our mother made us
turkey slices on a stick,
there'll be turkey tarts for supper,
all this turkey makes me sick.

For tomorrow she's preparing
turkey dumplings stuffed with peas,
oh I never thought I'd say this—
"Mother! No more turkey . . . PLEASE!"